CASEY JONES

Tale retold by Larry Dane Brimner
Illustrated by Drew Rose

Adviser: Dr. Alexa Sandmann, Professor of Literacy,
The University of Toledo; Member, International Reading Association

 COMPASS POINT BOOKS

Minneapolis, Minnesota

Compass Point Books
3109 West 50th Street, #115
Minneapolis, MN 55410

Visit Compass Point Books on the Internet at *www.compasspointbooks.com*
or e-mail your request to *custserv@compasspointbooks.com*

Dedication
For the kids of Rico, Colorado, and memories of its Galloping Goose.
    -LDB

Photographs ©: J. E. France, from the Bruce Gurner Collection,
Water Valley Casey Jones Railroad Museum, 28, 30.

Editor: Catherine Neitge
Photo Researcher: Svetlana Zhurkina
Designer: Les Tranby

Library of Congress Cataloging-in-Publication Data
The cataloging-in-publication data is on file with the Library of Congress.
ISBN 0-7565-0602-6
    2003019516

Table of Contents

The Greatest Engineer

Folks say Casey Jones was the greatest engineer who ever drove a train. Like almost every other hogger of the time, though, he was a daredevil. No other engineer had his special touch on the throttle. Why, Casey could highball an engine until the driver rods looked like one and the great steel wheels seemed to disappear. Trains just seemed to fly above the track whenever Casey was in the cab. He could push an engine to its limit until lost time was found, and he brought his train in on schedule.

"On time. Every time." That was Casey's motto.

Along the line, folks always knew when Casey was at the throttle. "Wooo…OOO…ooo!" He'd tickle the whistle in a special way until it warbled a mournful sound that spread out across the countryside.

"Must be Casey Jones in the cab," people would say, checking their clocks and pocket watches. "On time. Every time."

If the train was running on schedule and whistled like no other, it was indeed Casey Jones.

Getting His Start

Casey Jones was born to work for the railroad. He had no choice about it. The first sound he ever heard was the mournful tune of a passing locomotive whistle. The rumble of engines entering the nearby roundhouse rocked his cradle by day and sang him to sleep at night. A lot of people say that railroading was in his blood because his mama raised him on engine oil and mashed soot. Whatever the cause, all young Casey ever talked about was working for the railroad.

By the time he boarded his first train, he was ready for a rip-roaring rail adventure. That's just what he got.

That summer was the hottest on record. It was so hot that Georgia's Okefenokee Swamp had turned to desert. People in those parts were suffering something awful. They were hotter than grits on a griddle of sizzling fat. Casey reported to work one morning as usual. The stationmaster told him to take a train up to Minnesota to get some ice for those poor souls in Georgia.

Casey drove his engine hard. He arrived so far ahead of schedule that it was still winter in Minnesota. He picked up six freight cars of ice. Then he decided to nip next door to Wisconsin to pick up some milk, since his mama always seemed to be running low.

9

When Casey climbed into his cab for the return trip, he gave his special whistle: "Wooo…OOO…ooo." Then he eased on the throttle. Before long, the train was rocking and rolling, rolling and rocking down the rails.

"Keep her fed good," Casey called out to his fireman Sim Webb. That's just what Sim did.

The train zipped through Illinois. It raced through Kentucky. It rocketed through Tennessee. By the time it reached Georgia, it was flying above the track.

When Casey eased his train into the station, people from all parts crowded onto the station platform. Everyone wanted ice to cool their sweet tea and lemonade, and there was plenty to go around—four freight cars full.

The other two freight cars held a surprise for Casey. He'd stored the milk for his mama in them, and all that rocking and rolling—and chilling—had created some of the finest ice cream ever! Unless it's fiction, this here's a fact: It was Casey Jones who introduced ice cream to that great part of the country called the South.

Someone had the idea to whip in some local peaches to the frozen concoction. After that, people didn't much care how hot it was. They just scooped up another helping of ice cream and sat back to count fireflies.

On the way back home to Memphis, Casey took his time. Even so, his train arrived on schedule. The stationmaster was waiting on the platform when the train pulled in. "On time, every time," he said, snapping his pocket watch shut. Then Casey, Sim, and the stationmaster had some of that sweet, Georgia peach ice cream.

A Record-Setting Trip

Casey Jones arrived at the train yard one morning and found a new, black locomotive sitting on the tracks. "She's the biggest ever built," said the superintendent. He was Casey's boss.

Casey admired the locomotive. It was so shiny that he could see his own reflection. "She looks like a fine engine," he said. "A hogger would be proud to drive her."

"How would you like to be that hogger?" asked the superintendent.

It was a proposition that Casey didn't even have to ponder. "Sure would," he said quickly, before the superintendent could change his mind.

"Here's the deal," the superintendent said. "I have a score to settle with the folks in California. They have a hogger who holds the speed record on the line between Chicago and San Francisco. You break that record and this here engine's yours to drive for as long as you want."

"I'll do my best, sir," Casey said, and he headed for Chicago. The morning Casey pulled away from the Chicago train depot in Engine 638, the sky was heavy with threatening, dark clouds. "Looks bad," said Sim Webb.

It did, but Casey said, "I'm not worried."

Before long, they were in the thick of the storm. Thunder roared louder than the engine. Lightning zinged this way and that. In some places, mudslides swept over the tracks. Washouts in other places left the tracks suspended in air. Even so, Sim kept on shoveling coal and Casey kept on driving.

Suddenly, Sim cried out, "Will you look at that?"

Up ahead, it looked as if there was a blazing fire right in the middle of the tracks. Casey slowed the train to a crawl. As it approached the blaze, he knew at once what had happened.

"Lightning's struck the trestle over Skull Valley and set it ablaze," he said. Then in one swift motion, he brought the engine to a stop and reversed its direction.

"I guess we won't be setting any speed records on this run," Sim said, sounding disappointed.

"I'm not so sure of that," Casey said.

Casey backed that train up over 15 miles (24 kilometers) of track. Then he headed forward toward the blazing trestle again.

"Why don't we see what this engine's made of?" Casey said to Sim.

Sim understood. He began to shovel coal into the firebox. The faster he shoveled, the harder Casey pushed the engine. By the time they reached the blazing trestle again, the engine and cars were practically flying above the track.

"Brace yourself!" Casey hollered.

Then Engine 638 charged into the flames. As it did, the entire length of trestle fell into the valley below. You might think ol' Casey and Sim were goners, but nothing could be further from the truth. That shiny black engine and the cars it was pulling were highballing so fast that they flew through the air and came to rest on tracks at the opposite side of the valley. Then the train kept on going.

Casey drove it across the plains and over the mountains and into San Francisco in record-breaking time. After that, Casey broke speed records on nearly every run—until one fateful night in 1900.

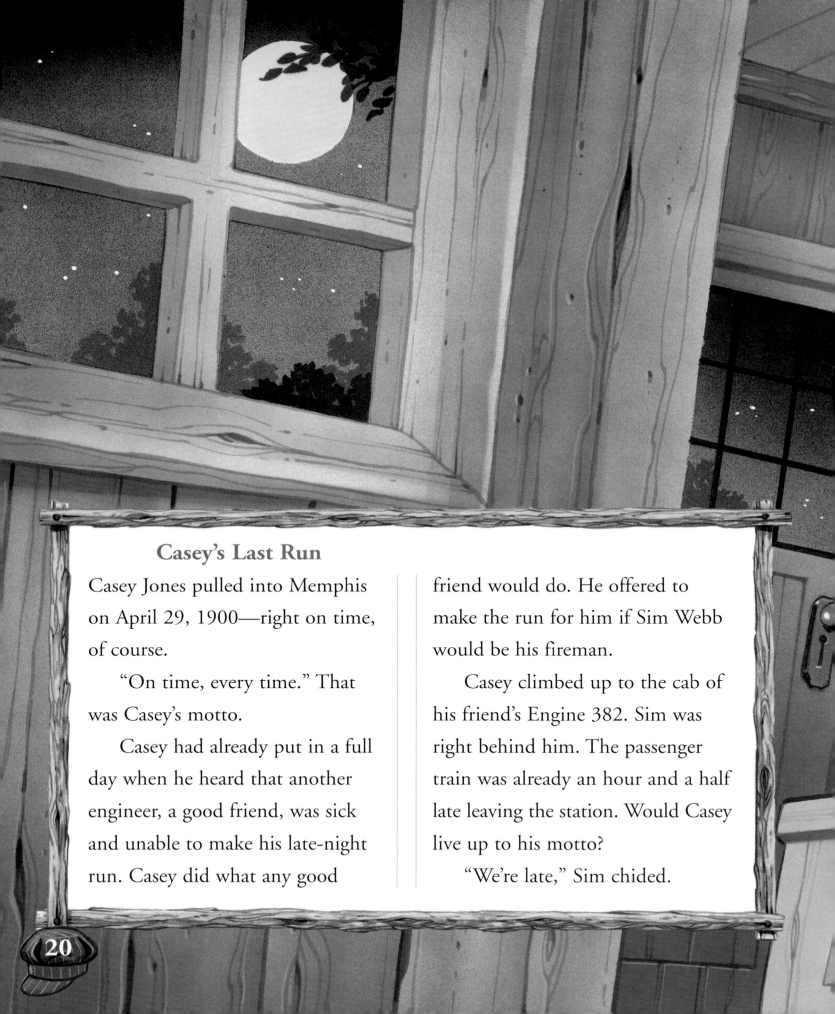

Casey's Last Run

Casey Jones pulled into Memphis on April 29, 1900—right on time, of course.

"On time, every time." That was Casey's motto.

Casey had already put in a full day when he heard that another engineer, a good friend, was sick and unable to make his late-night run. Casey did what any good friend would do. He offered to make the run for him if Sim Webb would be his fireman.

Casey climbed up to the cab of his friend's Engine 382. Sim was right behind him. The passenger train was already an hour and a half late leaving the station. Would Casey live up to his motto?

"We're late," Sim chided.

Casey nodded. "Yup, we're running late," he said, and tickled the train's whistle. "But I got me a good fireman. Got me a good engine. And heck, Sim, this ol' train's about as light as they come." Casey was thoughtful a minute, then he smiled. "Seems to me like perfect conditions to set another speed record."

Sim started shoveling. Casey started driving. Before long, Casey was highballing down the line, finding lost time. By 3:30 in the morning, he almost had the train back on schedule. Then disaster struck.

Near Vaughan, Mississippi, just as Casey rolled south around a bend, Sim let out a holler. "Train!"

Something wasn't right up ahead on the track. A freight train had pulled onto a passing track to let Engine 382 by, but it was stalled with several cars still on the main line. Casey pulled the brake lever with all his might, threw the engine into reverse, and blew the whistle until it screamed. It was no use. "Jump, Sim, and save yourself!" he called.

Ever since the night of that unfortunate wreck, people have sung "The Ballad of Casey Jones":

At 3:52 that morning came the fateful end,
Casey took his farewell trip to the promised land.
Casey Jones, he died at the throttle,
With the whistle in his hand.
Casey Jones, he died at the throttle,
But we'll all see Casey in the promised land.

The Real Casey Jones

1863 John Luther Jones was born in southwest Missouri on March 14; he moved to Cayce, Kentucky, as a boy and received the nickname Casey

1878 Moved to Columbus, Kentucky, to join the Mobile and Ohio Railroad

1886 Married Janie Brady in Jackson, Tennessee, where they spent most of their married life

1888 Joined the Illinois Central Railroad in Jackson

1900 Died on April 30 near Vaughan, Mississippi

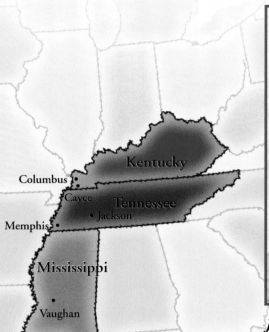

John Luther Jones, better known as Casey Jones

Becoming a Legend

The legend of Casey Jones has been around for more than 100 years. It started when a train worker named Wallace Saunders wrote a little ballad to honor Casey Jones after the horrible accident in 1900. Over the years, verses were added to the original, and the legend of Casey Jones grew until it became a tall tale.

It's true that investigators said that Casey was responsible for the accident that April night because he was driving too fast and failed to respond to flag signals. Casey will be remembered as a hero, though, because he saved the lives of the train's 300 passengers. Casey's actions also made it possible for Sim Webb to escape the wreck. That's just the sort of thing that turns an ordinary person into a legend—one fit for a tall tale.

Hobo Beans

With the arrival of trains came a new form of travel. Trains were used to move not only goods from one place to another but also people. While most people rode the rails in the comfort of passenger cars, others—mainly hoboes, or tramps—went without paying fares. They hopped into empty boxcars, riding to anyplace the tracks might lead them. Hoboes often got by with little or nothing, relying on handouts and what they could scrounge to survive. Here's a meal that would be sure to satisfy anyone in a hobo camp. Why, Casey Jones would have loved it himself! It serves 10.

2 pounds ground beef
1 large onion, chopped
3 16-ounce cans pork and beans
1 12-ounce jar chili sauce
1 8-ounce can crushed pineapple, drained

1 cup firmly packed dark brown sugar
1 tablespoon prepared mustard
1 tablespoon Worcestershire sauce
6 slices bacon, crisply cooked and crumbled

Combine the beef and onion in a large skillet. Brown the beef, stirring until it crumbles and the onion is transparent. Drain. Pour the beef mixture into a slow cooker. Add the remaining ingredients to the slow cooker and stir to combine. Cover and cook on high setting for 3 1/2 hours.

Glossary

ballad—a simple poem that tells a story and is sung

fireman—a person who tends the coal fire on a train engine

highball—to speed or go fast

hogger—a slang term for a train engineer

ponder—to consider or think about

roundhouse—a circular building that services and repairs locomotives

suspended—to hang

throttle—a lever, pedal, or handle used to control the speed of an engine

trestle—a framework that holds up a railroad bridge

Did You Know?

➤ Casey Jones's real name was John Luther Jones. He was nicknamed Casey by his crew because he was born near Cayce, Kentucky.

➤ Casey Jones was born in 1863. In 1886, he married Janie Brady. The couple had three children: Charles, Helen, and John Lloyd.

➤ Casey Jones appeared on a 3-cent United States postage stamp in 1950. Drawings of Casey Jones's engine appeared on two stamps from the small Pacific Island country of Tuvalu in the 1980s.

The real Casey Jones in an engine cab

Want to Know More?

At the Library

Cohn, Amy L. *From Sea to Shining Sea: A Treasury of American Folklore and Folk Songs.* New York: Scholastic, Inc., 1993.

Drummond, Allan. *Casey Jones.* New York: Farrar, Straus & Giroux, 2001.

Johnston, Marianne. *Casey Jones.* New York: Powerkids Press, 2001.

On the Web

For more information on *Casey Jones,* use FactHound to track down Web sites related to this book.

1. Go to *www.compasspointbooks.com/ facthound*
2. Type in this book ID: 0756506026
3. Click on the *Fetch It* button.

Your trusty FactHound will fetch the best Web sites for you!

Through the Mail

The Water Valley Casey Jones Railroad Museum
105 Railroad Ave.
Water Valley, MS 38965
662/473-3828
To write for information about the life of Casey Jones

On the Road

Casey Jones Home and Railroad Village
56 Casey Jones Lane
Jackson, TN 38305
800/748-9588
To visit a museum that includes Casey's house, a steam engine similar to Casey's Engine 638, and other details about the life and death of America's greatest railroad engineer

Casey Jones Railroad Museum State Park
Vaughan, MS 39179
662/673-9864
To visit a museum that houses railroad artifacts, including the bell from Engine 382

Index

About the Author
Larry Dane Brimner has written more than 100 books for young people, including the award-winning *Merry Christmas, Old Armadillo* (Boyds Mills Press) and *The Littlest Wolf* (HarperCollins Publishers). He is also the reteller of several other Tall Tales, including *Calamity Jane, Captain Stormalong, Davy Crockett,* and *Molly Pitcher*. Sometimes Mr. Brimner can hear the lonely wails of trains as they pass through Tucson, Arizona, where he makes his home.

About the Illustrator
Drew Rose spent many afternoons of his childhood enjoying the illustrations in books at the library. Now he is happy to help other stories come to life with his own art. He is also the illustrator of another Tall Tale, *John Henry*. His wife, Tricia, and their two cats, Iris and Micetro, live with him in Atlanta, Georgia.